# CURING MARXISM

## A Crippling and Deadly Disease

RYAN L. ROBINSON

Word Art Publishing
9350 Wilshire Blvd
Suite 203, Beverly Hills, CA 90212
www.wordartpublishing.com
Phone: 1 (888) 614 - 1370



Published by Word Art Publishing

ISBN:  Paperback    978-1-955070-48-5
       Hardback     978-1-955070-49-2
       Ebook        978-1-955070-50-8

THIS BOOK IS DEDICATED TO:

The 100 million people who died at the hands of
the Marxist in the last century.
My Family for putting up with my nonsense.
The ones who have fallen; Bob, Vivian, Jan, and Hal.
To Tree and JoAnn, for making this book much better.
A special thanks to the late Hal Fisher and Dr. Marcel Methot
on keeping me centered on what was important.

# TABLE OF CONTENTS


Preface . . . . . . . . . . . . . . . . . . . . . . . . . . . . . . . . . . . . . . . . . . . . .vii

A Crippling and Deadly Disease . . . . . . . . . . . . . . . . . . . . . . . ix

Plank #1 . . . . . . . . . . . . . . . . . . . . . . . . . . . . . . . . . . . . . . . .1

Plank #2 . . . . . . . . . . . . . . . . . . . . . . . . . . . . . . . . . . . . . . .6

Plank #3 . . . . . . . . . . . . . . . . . . . . . . . . . . . . . . . . . . . . . .10

Plank #4 . . . . . . . . . . . . . . . . . . . . . . . . . . . . . . . . . . . . . .14

Plank #5 . . . . . . . . . . . . . . . . . . . . . . . . . . . . . . . . . . . . . .18

Plank #6 . . . . . . . . . . . . . . . . . . . . . . . . . . . . . . . . . . . . . .25

Plank #7 . . . . . . . . . . . . . . . . . . . . . . . . . . . . . . . . . . . . . .31

Plank #8 . . . . . . . . . . . . . . . . . . . . . . . . . . . . . . . . . . . . . .38

Plank #9 . . . . . . . . . . . . . . . . . . . . . . . . . . . . . . . . . . . . . .43

Plank #10 . . . . . . . . . . . . . . . . . . . . . . . . . . . . . . . . . . . . .47

Combining Planks for Amendments . . . . . . . . . . . . . . . . . . . .52

Is this the End? . . . . . . . . . . . . . . . . . . . . . . . . . . . . . . . . .60

Notes . . . . . . . . . . . . . . . . . . . . . . . . . . . . . . . . . . . . . . . .63

# PREFACE

"Freedom is fraught with danger.   Socialism, Marxism, Fascism, Communism, Naziism . . . You get the idea."

Melvin Entwhistle

This book is a manifestation of my personal ideas and concerns to protect the United States from some of the evils of the world.  If you are one of the following:

Socialist
Marxist
Leninist
Fascist
Communist
Or a Nazi

Put the book back on the shelf and leave it alone.  This book is for freedom loving people.  I forbid you from reading this book; you are not allowed.

Ryan L. Robinson

# A CRIPPLING AND DEADLY DISEASE

What is this about a disease? I'm writing this in 2022, the era of Covid-19. Getting a shot was all the buzz in the media. There was a lot of controversy about the Covid-19. This all may be true, but don't get overly hung up on it because many diseases like polio and Measles have been defeated by vaccines. I thought the principle of defeating a disease would be the perfect analogy or metaphor for this book.

You see, the disease is Marxism or Socialism. The whole purpose of this book is to open some ideas for discussion and expose them to the light of day. So please bear with me and let's get started.

What is Socialism? There is both an economic and political aspect to socialism. If you combine the two, you get a collective or group ownership of all production and distribution of goods and services. To pull this off the government must eliminate private property and your freedom and liberty.

You might ask, if everybody owns everything under Socialism, does everyone run and make the decisions about everything? No, of course not. We all have our own opinions. You couldn't expect everyone to make the critical decisions to run a business. With Socialism that is left up to the elites. That is a group of wiser, well connected, and a whole lot more deserving than you (or so they would have you believe). [1]

To shorten it up, "The government owns and runs everything, and you own and run nothing."

So, what's wrong with Socialism? I liked what Churchill said about Socialism, that it is the philosophy of failure, the creed of ignorance, and the gospel of envy. [2]

Socialism has failed all over the world and is continuing to fail in places like Venezuela and Cuba. It doesn't take much to see the difference between these countries and the economic success of a free market country. It is not just the freedom but the sheer body count that matters. That is what I'm most concerned with. Look at the death toll from the last century and the millions that have died [3] under the 'creed of ignorance.'

If we look at the Peoples Republic of China, some 65 million people died at the hands of the Great Leap Forward, later called the Cultural Revolution. The Soviet Union did much better with only around 30 million dead. Cambodia is another victim. I have heard anywhere from 2 to 6 million died under Pol Pots' Khmer Rouge revolution. And that is just the top of the list.

The data varies, but it is generally estimated that the century between 1900 and 2000, at least 100 million people have died directly from these infectious ideas of Marxism and Socialism.

You might ask, "why did they die?" Let's take Cambodia as an example. When Pol Pot came into power, any Cambodians suspected of being disloyal were shot right away. If you were smart or educated like doctors, lawyers, journalists, teachers, wore glasses or perceived to be intellectuals. You were shot.

What was wrong with wearing glasses? If you wore glasses, you could read. If you could read, you were educated. If you were educated, you were an intellectual. Bang, bang.

They forced millions of people out of their homes and onto collective farms where they were worked to death. Advanced mechanisms like cars were broken down and melted into buckets. [4] Many who weren't killed outright died of starvation.

This is not my idea of a good way to spend the summer.

Another question that might be asked, is Marxism still around or even a threat? I assure you that it is alive and well in this country and many others. It has endeavored to change its stripes and labels, but it is still here. And it is not going away. That is why we as a country and people must stifle its presence. And that is why I'm writing this book.

Throughout this work I use the term's Socialism, Marxism, Fascism and Communism almost interchangeably. There are technical differences between them, of course, but they are basically the same, totalitarianism at its worst. The discussion above does not show the millions that died from the Fascist in WWII. Some might believe that Nazis are the opposites of Communist; one is on the left and the other is on the right. I reject this idea it is not totally true. Sometimes you can get to the same place by two different roads. You see, 'NAZI' stands for 'National <u>Socialist</u> German Workers' Party. They both have the same goals, totalitarianism over freedom and the state over the people or individuals.

But if that were the case then why did the Russians and Germans fight each other during WWII if they were the same? For the same reason sibling's fight.

"Mommy, Sis got more mashed potatoes than I did!"

It was probably more like, "I can take Poland before you can!"

Socialism is Socialism and truly an idea that can kill.

Most people don't think about a social-economic system as a disease. Some social-economic practices are good, like the classic generosity towards the disadvantaged during Christmas and some are very bad like fascism. So, let's look at the similarities between these and biological diseases.

The idea of Marxism rests in an infected organism (an ordinary person). The organism meets with another of its kind (another person), and through interaction (talking and body language) infects the new organism to become a carrier of the disease (excites them about the wondrous possibilities of Marxism). The newly infected organism goes out and meets with another new organism (another person) and the idea spreads. That sounds like an infection to me.

Ever since 1848, when Karl Heinrich Marx and Friedrich Engels wrote the Communist Manifesto, the people of the world have been plagued by the hideous attempts of others to restructure their societies into this regimented and rigorous (and deadly) form. This configuration may work well for ants or bees or space aliens but is not fit for humans. The failures of Marxism and Socialism have piled up bodies ever since. This is not only at the hands of the Socialist leaders but the policies that brought hunger and starvation to their people. The exact number can be researched and debated, but that is not the point of this writing. The bottom line is that Marxism, Fascism, Communism, and socialism are all very, very bad. In fact, they are stupid; classic Carlo Cipolla [5] type of stupid. This type of stupid means that it not only hurts the common followers of these philosophies, but it also hurts the elites who believe they should direct the affairs of a country. These elites often wind up in a well deserving grave, like Pol Pot.

As for the common revolutionary, I believe that is why the Marxist and Communist elites call them 'useful idiots'. This term is directed at the masses at the bottom of the heap by the elites at the top. [6]

The real question is how do you prevent it from becoming a malignancy in your country? The drive to make the USA into an extreme Socialist country has been deliberate and methodical. The American people have been like contented Jack Rabbits. They have been jumping around from one shiny thing to another and minding their own business and family and enjoying a lot of what this great country has to offer. We hoped this would be the benefit of living in a free society. It is. And this is good, but only if we continue to be vigilant.

The socialists, on the other hand, have been slower but more accurate to put in place the changes required to accomplish what they needed done. This is a patient and deliberate approach, much like a tortoise. And we all know who wins the race between the tortoise and the hare.

> "The American people will never knowingly adopt socialism, but under the name of liberalism they will adopt every fragment of the socialist program until one day America will be a socialist nation without ever knowing how it happened." [7]
>
> – Norman Thomas 1944

Do I have to make the jump for you? Can you see the base roots to what Biden's adviser meant? He said, 'This is about the future of the Liberal World Order.' And what did he really mean? Is it as simple as replacing 'Liberal' with 'Socialist' or 'Communist'? I believe so.

I believe there are two things, if brought together, could act as a stabilizing mechanism or vaccine for our republic. The first is the Bill of Rights. Although it has been much debated, the Bill of Rights has laid down the inalienable rights of the people and to protect them from aspects with respect to the government. Remember the Bill of Rights is a contract between "We the People" and our government to protect us from a tyrannical government like we experienced with England. Things like the First Amendment, freedom of speech, freedom of religion, freedom to assemble, the Second Amendment, the right to keep and bear arms, the Third Amendment, . . . You get the idea. And we should always think and speak of the Bill of Rights as unchangeable absolutes. The Bill of Rights has done its job well and has kept us free from monarchs and dictatorships, the threats of that time. It has done so for some two hundred and thirty years. Marxism and Communism had not been invented in 1791 when the Bill of Rights was written. Now this new plague is upon us, and we need a booster shot.

A vaccine is created by taking the disease or dead parts of it and manipulating it in such a way as to produce the vaccine that fights the infection. I am not a chemist or biologist, but this is my basic understanding. The sample of the disease we are concerned with would be found in the Marxist requirements, for the conversion of the country to Communism.

Karl Marx wrote ten "Planks," or political declaration in the Communist Manifesto, what we should consider as the requirements to infect a society. These "Planks" must not be allowed to happen; or remove them if they are already in place. We therefore must take the "planks", or the dead parts of the disease, manipulate these parts, and put them in a mechanism to prevent the disease from causing harm. In other words, a vaccine.

I will go over each plank, identify what is wrong with the plank and some of the ideas adopted by America to support them. I will then define what elements we need protection from, and what is needed as an amendment to secure it into law.

I admit that in some cases, I found the "Plank" or idea sounded reasonable. It might have been an idea or policy I grew up with. It may be a policy that doesn't appear threatening. But in other cases, I found the planks downright immoral. I'm basing this all on an article posted on the internet.

"The Ten Planks of the Communist Manifesto BY TS on AUGUST 5, 2016." [8]

This article was originally posted at Laissez-Faire Republic

A new set of Constitutional Amendments would hopefully help and support The Bill of Rights to preserve our freedom and domestic tyranny. I call this set of Amendments, The Bill of Additional Rights. I said that some of these planks didn't appear threatening. Why would we need an Amendment? To make them absolute and protect us in the future.

I must emphasize that I'm not a constitutional lawyer and some of the wording may not be perfect. Remember, I'm trying to expose an idea to the light of day for discussion. An idea should be hammered out into a legal defense against a most deadly tyranny.

I believe the solution is simple, but by no means easy.

# PLANK ONE

The Ten Planks from the Communist Manifesto 1848 by Karl Heinrich Marx & Friedrich Engels

Plank #1
Abolition of private property in land and application of all rents of land to public purpose.

# WHAT IS WRONG WITH PLANK ONE?

Why would the government want to abolish private property? The only reason I can think of is to control it and use it for their own purposes. Sometimes this is a noble endeavor like building a military base or a highway extension. These and other projects are beneficial for the country and the people in those areas surrounding the improvements. This is usually carried out with "eminent domain."[9]

Eminent domain is the power of the federal, state, and local governments to take private property for public use. This is, of course, after the payment of just compensation. [10]

What concerns me is the term 'just compensation.' There is a basic moral law that is hard to get away from. Simply put, "You shall not steal." [11] 'Eminent domain' could be considered stealing. Especially if a person doesn't want to sell his/her property 'just' for some kind of 'compensation'.

Unfortunately, even under the best of conditions this can be very susceptible to corruption and graft.

For example: A business wants a building downtown to expand its operation. This expansion will increase tourism for the community and will benefit everyone. Let's say that some people like their community the way it is and do not want the expansion. Maybe the owner of the building does not want to sell. The confiscation of the building, or forced selling, can be accomplished many ways. Eminent domain is just one. Various zoning regulations, land use regulations, property taxes, and environmental laws are but a few other ways to force this issue.

Community leaders don't always have to be bribed to take this action. They may think that it's good for the community, as well as benefitting them.

Sometimes the disrespect for property leads to disrespect of people. As a Founding Father, John Adams said: "The moment the idea is admitted into society that property is not as sacred as the law of God, and that there is not a force of law and public justice to protect it, anarchy and tyranny commence." [12]

This reminds me of the riots in 2020 and 2021, anarchy and tyranny ruled, and other people's property was not respected and burned to the ground.

## WHAT ADDITIONAL CONSIDERATIONS SHOULD BE RESOLVED?

- Eminent domain

  Everything you can own is subject to "eminent domain." Things like land, contract rights, airspace, mineral rights, and the last book you published is subject to eminent domain. And they can take it away from you by <u>usurping private property</u> for public use. And of course, giving you <u>fair compensation</u> for your trouble. [13]

  A person may not want his intellectual property shared with the world or give up his/her property. The key here is 'fair compensation' and 'usurp.' Most of us have an idea what 'fair compensation' means. Unfortunately, the people handing out the fair compensation may have other ideas of how much is fair.

  'Usurp,' on the other hand, means taking illegally or by force. [14] To say the least, in the United States, property is sometimes taken by force. This is simply wrong, and we should make it 'illegal.'

- Forfeiture provisions of the RICO statutes

  RICO is the Racketeer Influenced and Corrupt Organizations Act. This is when a defendant engages in two or more instances of racketeering activity. Where a defendant directly invested in, maintained an interest in, or participated in a criminal enterprise affecting interstate or foreign commerce. [15]

  This should only apply to money and properties obtained illegally. It should not apply to property they owned before the criminal activity.

- Various zoning regulations

    Zoning laws are usually intended to organize a developing city. Can it be used to obtain property? I'm sure it has. But that is not right. Perhaps we should make it harder to confiscate property using zoning laws.

- Environmental concerns and Land use regulations

    The National Environmental Policy Act, or (NEPA), was set up to promote the general welfare, and maintain conditions for man and nature to exist in harmony. This effort includes social, financial, and technical assistance. The hope is to meet the requirements of present and future generations of Americans. [16]

    This sounds good and reasonable. If we are keeping toxic waste out of rivers and the rivers out of toxic waste and pollution out of the air, I'm all for it. This is a noble endeavor and benefits everyone. If, on the other hand, this is used to move property from one person to another and there is no danger, then it's criminal.

There are many agencies that are part of the federal, state, and local governments that have influence over our lives. Many of these are applicable to this writing. I will address others in later chapters. If I leave out your favorite, I apologize.

## WHAT WE NEED TO COUNTER, TO PROTECT THE PEOPLE.

- Eminent domain
- Forfeiture provisions
- Abolishment of private property

Our private property belongs to us and can't be taken away on a whim by the government or anyone else unless they have a very good reason.

# BILL OF ADDITIONAL RIGHTS AMENDMENT

*Amendment*

*Section 1.*

*Federal, State, and local, governments shall not abolish private property.*

*Section 2.*

*Federal, State, and local, governments or their agencies, shall not confiscate private property or use 'eminent domain' to obtain property for private use. It must be for government use only and paid for at fair market prices. If the property is not used for the original government purpose within four years, the property is returned to the previous owner without charge.*

*Section 3.*

*Federal, State, and local, governments can only confiscate private property under 'Forfeiture' provisions if that property has been obtained illegally.*

# PLANK TWO

The Ten Planks from the Communist Manifesto
1848 by Karl Heinrich Marx & Friedrich Engels

Plank #2
A heavy progressive or graduated income tax.

# WHAT IS WRONG WITH PLANK TWO?

No one likes taxes. What is so bad about a graduated income tax? A graduated income tax is what the U.S. uses, and it changes the percentage of tax you pay as you make more money. As an example, a person making $25,000/yr. may be taxed at 10% and would pay $2,500. Another person making $250,000/yr. might be taxed a 30%, would pay $75,000.

I think this system treats different people differently and in the long-run, consistency is fair. Everybody in the same country should be treated the same way, especially in America. But that's not all, these taxes take away capital for future growth, job creation, and salary increases.

The best alternative would be to not have taxes. Some states don't have income taxes. However wonderful and ideal that would be, I think it would be a difficult transition at the federal level. What would be some alternative to a graduated income tax?

Historically tariffs have served a key role in the trade policy of the United States. But to start with, their purpose was to generate revenue for the federal government. [17] This dual function of tariffs makes it more complicated to balance trade policy and revenue. You may need more money but can't afford to upset other countries. There must be something better.

The "flat tax." [18] A flat tax imposes the same tax rate to every 'taxpayer' with no regard of income level. If the tax rate is 10%, a person making $25,000/yr. would pay $2,500. Another person making $250,000/yr. would pay $25,000. And remember, this should be implemented without any deductions or loopholes. There are many pros and cons and other aspects to consider with this type of tax.

Some people believe that a flat tax should not apply to the very poor. I tend to agree with this. A decision would have to be made, at what income level would a person become a 'taxpayer' and at what overall tax rate would apply. This starting level would change over the years as conditions change. As an example, you might say that taxpayers start at making more than $30,000 a year and the flat tax will be 12%.

The starting point and percentage of tax would change depending on the economic conditions and the situations in the country.

This would certainly make filling out your tax's easier and would be cheaper to do the paperwork. Most people could do it themselves. In fact, there would be less work for the IRS to do. We could de-fund and re-imagine the IRS, saving the taxpayers a lot of money.

Just a side note. I would love to see the IRS put to a more practical endeavor, like doing a forensic audit on politicians and their families before and after each term of office. There is no place for corruption in America.

The plank said 'heavy progressive' tax. Maybe we could just remove the term 'heavy'. But what is 'heavy?' What may seem heavy during a prosperous stretch in a future history may be grossly insufficient during a war for the nation's survival. 'Heavy' can only be defined at an instant in time. This will not work and should not be considered.

So, I'm in favor of a 'flat tax.' It's not so much that I like flat taxes. It's that Marxists don't like them.

## WHAT ADDITIONAL CONSIDERATIONS SHOULD BE RESOLVED?

- The 16$^{th}$ amendment gives the government the right to tax our income.

AMENDMENT XVI
Passed by Congress July 2, 1909.
Ratified February 3, 1913.

Note: Article I, section 9, of the Constitution was modified by amendment 16.

The Congress shall have power to lay and collect taxes on incomes, from whatever source derived, without apportionment among the several States, and without regard to any census or enumeration.

So, this amendment made it legal to tax income. This would have been a good place to require a 'flat tax' only.

# WHAT WE NEED TO COUNTER,
# TO PROTECT THE PEOPLE.

- Progressive income tax
- Graduated income tax

Taxes must be fair and reasonable.

## BILL OF ADDITIONAL RIGHTS AMENDMENT

*Amendment*
 *No Federal, State, or local governments shall establish a progressive or graduated tax.*

# PLANK THREE

The Ten Planks from the Communist Manifesto
1848 by Karl Heinrich Marx & Friedrich Engels

Plank #3
Abolition of all rights of inheritance.

# WHAT IS WRONG WITH PLANK THREE?

This is part of the Marxist destruction and elimination of private property. It says that you can't give property to anyone when you die and you can't receive any property when someone else, like your mother or father dies. Children are a big part of most people's life, as it should be. You want the best for them, to live better, to be happier and more successful than you. A good way for most people to help with this is through inheritance.

The Marxists don't like this. They have no control, and the horror stories write themselves. A family heirloom is ripped away from a grieving woman whose mother has just died. A young man working the family farm and providing for his new family is told that the land now belongs to the state; it's okay, however, because he will continue to work on the land. The new supervisor, the mayor's brother, will be there tomorrow to take control. You get the idea, a fertile ground for corruption.

Government has been encroaching on this for a while, mostly in the form of taxes.

## WHAT ADDITIONAL CONSIDERATIONS SHOULD BE RESOLVED?

- Federal & State Estate Taxes (1916)

    An estate tax is when the government taxes the total value of the deceased person's money and property <u>before</u> any of the decedent's assets are distributed. [19]

    If the estate is taxed before distribution, there is a chance that tax would be at a higher rate (see the previous plank on graduated income tax) then if it was done after distribution. This is especially true if there were more than one person receiving the inheritance.

- Inheritance Taxes

    An inheritance tax is applied to the estate after it has been divided and distributed. The tax is calculated separately for each individual who receives the inheritance, and they must pay the tax. [20]

These have eliminated or greatly diluted the right of private property owners to determine the disposition and distribution of their estates upon their death. The moral question is, does the state or federal government have a right to infringe on an individual to do this? I say, no.

There is one place where both, Estate Taxes and Inheritance Taxes apply, Maryland. Double taxation. That is very wrong.

- Historical Precedence

    A long time ago, all inheritance went to the oldest son. That was the extent of the discussion. In this more modern time things have gotten more complicated. We should leave it up to the person who owns the property to make that judgment. We have developed an elaborate document to do this incredibly complicated task. It's called, a Will.

- Criminal Activities

    A person should not have the right to pass on criminally obtained property to another person. If you stole the property, you must give it back. To prevent criminal activity and defend the rights of the individual, the correct due process must be performed.

- Legal Obligations

    The person that owns the property could have liens, debts, or financial obligations at the time of his passing. Are these also inherited by the recipient of the property or is the financial obligation taken care of before the recipient receives the property? The recipient may benefit one way or the other. This may have to be resolved on individual situations by state law and/or the courts.

# WHAT WE NEED TO COUNTER, TO PROTECT THE PEOPLE.

- Taxation of inheritance
- Abolition of inheritance
- Abolition to give an inheritance
- Abolition to get an inheritance
- Lack of legal Obligations of inheritance

We cannot allow the abolition or control of inheritance by the state. They didn't earn it and have no business meddling with it.

## BILL OF ADDITIONAL RIGHTS AMENDMENT

*Amendment*

*No seizure or taxation or abolition of the rights to give or receive inheritance shall be made without legal due process and only if it is involved in an illegal act.*

# PLANK FOUR

The Ten Planks from the Communist Manifesto 1848 by Karl Heinrich Marx & Friedrich Engels

Plank #4
Confiscation of the property of all emigrants and rebels.

## WHAT IS WRONG WITH PLANK FOUR?

Again, we see Marxist wanting to confiscate private property. This at the basic level is immoral. I'm not sure why they are picking on emigrants. Other than a few contraband items, we allow legal emigrants to bring in their belongings. This is reasonable and fair.

Rebels on the other hand are a different matter. Some rebels we might applaud and others arrest. A better term for a "rebel" we would arrest might be "criminal." Contraband and illegally obtained items should be confiscated.

It is wrong to forcibly take legally obtained property from anyone unless the property itself is illegal.

## WHAT ADDITIONAL CONSIDERATIONS SHOULD BE RESOLVED?

- Government seizures and "Forfeiture"

  We looked at these in Plank 1. I'll restate the obvious. This should only apply to money and properties obtained illegally. This should not apply to property they owned before the criminal activity. But this is not where it ends. Abuse of these revenues is stark corruption.

  Revenues generated through forfeiture have been spent with virtually no oversight. These funds reserved for 'law enforcement purposes' wind up getting spent on margarita machines, training trips to Hawaii, and chrome accents for Harley Davidson motorcycles.

  As one of our Founding Fathers, George Mason, put it, "When the same man, or set of men, holds the sword and the purse, there is an end of liberty." De-funding forfeitures is a good first step. [21]

  This practice must stop; it is basically immoral.

- Public 'law' 99-570 (1986)

  This Act of Congress made money laundering a federal crime. Section 1956 prohibits individuals from engaging in a financial transaction with proceeds that were generated from certain specific crimes. Additionally, the law requires that an individual specifically intent on making the transaction to conceal the source, ownership, or control of the funds. [22]

As I said before, you can't keep what you got illegally.

- 1997 Crime/Terrorist Bill

    As I stated before, terrorists are criminals and should be treated as criminals.

- IRS confiscation of property without due process

    If you neglect or refuse to fully pay your tax debt, the IRS can take your property. All the IRS has to do is file a public document, the Notice of Federal Tax Lien. This alerts creditors that the government has a legal right to your property. [23]

    See the following, 'Tax liens.'

- Tax liens

    A federal tax lien is the government's legal claim against your property and protects the government's interest. Fail to pay your taxes the lien helps the IRS to take your property, including real estate, personal and financial assets. [24]

    This, and the previous 'IRS confiscation', seems like government overreach. Any other organization that is due money can't do this without going through a court process.

    Individuals can collect on an unpaid debt by placing a lien against the debts' property. However, placing a lien against property takes large amounts of leg work and time in court. [25]

    The government should have to go through the same process as everyone else.

- Imprisonment of 'terrorists'

    Again, terrorists should be treated as any other criminal, fairly and with due process.

# WHAT WE NEED TO COUNTER, TO PROTECT THE PEOPLE.

- Confiscation of property from emigrants
- Confiscation of property from rebels (criminals)

We are a gracious country and should treat everyone like we would treat ourselves.

## BILL OF ADDITIONAL RIGHTS AMENDMENT

*Amendment*

*No Federal, State, or local, governments or their agencies shall confiscate property of immigrants or criminals without due process and only if the property has been proven to be involved in an illegal act.*

# PLANK FIVE

The Ten Planks from the Communist Manifesto
1848 by Karl Heinrich Marx & Friedrich Engels

Plank #5
Centralization of credit in the hands of the state,
by means of a national bank with state capital
and an exclusive monopoly.

# WHAT IS WRONG WITH PLANK FIVE?

What is a dollar?

The Federal Reserve System (known as the FED) is the central bank of the United States. What is wrong with a central bank? Vladimir Lenin said, "The establishment of a central bank is 90% of Communizing a nation." Ninety percent is a lot. This may be important.

The FED is not the only national bank we've had in our history. In fact, it is the third. The First Bank was a private bank chartered by Congress. The Second Bank resulted in a famous bank crisis with President Andrew Jackson. [26]

We seldom think about the FED unless the economy goes sideways, like with inflation. But we all need a bank, right? Or do we? What is wrong with this one?

To start with, the FED is not part of the U.S. government. [27] It's a private corporation. Also, our money is not representative money based on silver or gold or anything of value as it was at one time. Now our dollar (or Federal Reserve note) is not a dollar. The paper note from the FED is a term to describe 'the demand liabilities of the Federal Reserve.' [28] Whatever that means. For this and many other reasons I believe the FED is an obsolete and outdated relic.

This money, not based on anything of value, is called 'Fiat.' This 'Fiat' money under a central control becomes more worthless over time. 'Fiat' money is always at risk from inflation. If too much money is printed by the government, the value of the currency becomes less. [29] The 'Fiat' system must be reset, after so many years. This reset is a blessing to the Marxist or Socialist. This gives them some control.

As I said we have had three banks but there have been long gaps between them. We have done well without a state bank before, and I think we can live without it again.

The printing of money has long been an addiction of governments trying to make things 'better' for the nation and themselves. This has led to all sorts of economic woes, inflation being most common. If inflation is not kept at a low rate, you find yourself taking a wheelbarrow full of money to buy breakfast. Recent examples of this kind of inflation can be found in Germany during the great depression and Venezuela more recently. And as of the writing of this book, inflation in the U.S. is hovering around 8% to 9%.

As my good friend, Melvin Entwistle once said, "If you ignore the invisible hand, it will slap you silly."

The metaphor of the invisible hand is that unseen force that moves the free market economy. *30* The meaning is clear, if you don't understand the free market and make bad choices, you may have unwanted consequences.

Even by not printing a lot of money, there are ways things can go way out of control. In the late 1800s and early 1900s, many banks used to print their own money. By the end of the Civil War, an estimated one third of all the currency in the U.S. was counterfeit. [31] The government had no standards or control over what the currency looked like. If you got money from a bank in Boston and then went to El Paso, you might have to convince the good people of El Paso the money was real, and you could pay for your purchases.

So, what can you do to keep the government or anybody else from messing with the money? First it must be based on something real, like gold, or what is called representative money. The appeal of representative money is that it is not as susceptible to inflation. A government is only able to print enough money for the amount of gold they hold in their vaults. [32] When the money was based on gold, the system seemed to work well. Do we have enough gold today?

The chart below shows the amount of gold in our three main gold reserves.

| How much gold? | | Book Value | Current price | Value from debt clock |
|---|---|---|---|---|
| Gold Reserves | Troy Ounces of Gold | $42.22 per ounce. | $1,660.00 per ounce | $21,166 per ounce |
| Fort Knox, KY | 147,341,858.38 | $6,221,097,412.78 | $244,587,484,914.12 | $3,118,637,774,513.41 |
| West Point, NY | 54,067,331.38 | $2,282,841,677.17 | $89,751,770,089.14 | $1,144,389,135,967.91 |
| Denver, CO | 43,853,707.28 | $1,851,599,995.81 | $72,797,154,083.14 | $928,207,568,267.31 |
| total | 245,262,897.04 | $10,355,539,085.76 | $407,136,409,086.40 | $5,191,234,478,748.64 |

Here are millions of ounces of gold. The book value is what the gold is valued at by the U.S. Mint. The $1,660 per ounce is around the market price as of the writing of this book. The $21,166 per ounce is the price as of the US Debt Clock, approximately $5 Trillion. [33] There may not be enough to cover the approximate $20 Trillion needed to cover the M2 money supply. M2 money supply is the total money people can access quickly without penalties. Maybe a dollar could be backed by a fraction of a dollar worth of gold, like 10 percent (10 cent worth of gold) or 1 percent (1 cent worth of gold). And this might be a bad idea. It would be too easy for the government to dilute the value of the dollar (as described above). This is how civilizations collapse.

Here is another idea. The federal government owns about 640 million acres of land in the United States. 1 Acre = 4840 Square Yards. That is 3,097,600,000,000 (3 trillion) Square Yards. Have one dollar equal one Square Yard of the United States of America. Or back a dollar with one square foot of that land. That would be nine times the number of square yards or 27,878,400,000,000 (27 trillion) square feet. Have the money be backed by literally the country itself.

Although this could be diluted, the US could set aside a parcel of land and not add to it. You have no idea where your square foot is located, the top of Mt Hood or the Northeast corner of Area 51? You could never give dirt for a dollar just like we stopped giving out gold for the paper money. You wouldn't want someone giving the bank $43,560.00 and saying, "Where is my acre of land?" Although you could say that 5 square feet are in Alaska and 3 square feet are in the everglades and 8 square feet are . . . Well, you get the idea.

The implementation of this new currency should also be updated. A decentralized non programable block-chain crypto currency, very similar to Bitcoin would work. Perhaps twenty trillion dollars market cap would be the right size (maybe more). Using a debit card for payment is very common for people these days. Linking your local bank accounts' debit card or your digital wallet to this new, let's call it, 'Greenback Coin' would be very convenient and make it easy for people to transition.

When I say 'decentralized' and 'non programable' I mean that no one controls the value or use of the new 'Greenback Coin'. I'm not an economist but my understanding is that as the country grew and prospered, the 'Greenback Coin' currency would grow more valuable, not less.

On the other hand, dollars could be centralized, serialized, programable, and non-crypto digital currency, like proposed by the FED. This is called Central Bank Digital Currency or CBDC. This money is easy to track and could be assigned usage or frozen. So, when I say 'crypto,' I mean that no one can manipulate the block-chain and direct the usage of that dollar or change it.

It is too inviting for (Marxist or any other) governments to put limitations on some ones centralized non crypto programable digital money (CBDC) for the governments purpose.

For example: The government might say, "You haven't spent any money at local business. We have designated 10% of your money to be spent at only local business. Here is a list we suggest." And 10% of your money won't spend anywhere else. Or it won't spend over ten miles from your house.

Another example: "You can't buy a new car," The government might say. "You spend too much on beer. But here is a list of used models you are permitted to buy."

Another example: What did Prime Minister Trudeau of Canada do to the demonstrating truckers? He froze their bank accounts, and they couldn't get to their money. It would be easier to do this with digital money and wouldn't require the banks involvement and the money just wouldn't spend. They could even assign your money to someone else. Marxists love this kind of control over the economy and you. You might as well put on the collar and hand them the leash.

Another possibility is to just outright adopt Bitcoin or another existing crypto currency and have that as the coin of the realm. This would be the simplest and quickest way to implement this change. Also, it would not be using 'state capital' as mentioned in the plank.

Would these changes make a smooth-running economy? No, of course not. There would be problems along the way, but in the long term, the hick-ups would be much less severe. And the solutions would be equitable for all. Although, money is not free, our money must be free from manipulation by evil and self-righteous people.

By the way, a dollar was defined by Congress in 1787, as 375.64 grains of fine Silver. At the time of the writing of this book, silver is approximately $19 per oz (in FED dollars). That would make the dollar of 1787 worth around $16.30 in 'demand liabilities of the Federal Reserve.' Has the dollar of 1787 increased in value or has the FED note decreased in value?

## WHAT ADDITIONAL CONSIDERATIONS SHOULD BE RESOLVED?

- Federal Reserve Act of Congress in 1913

   The purpose of this act was to give the nation a safer, more flexible, and more stable financial system. To accomplish this would require free market intervention. This kind of intervention would include Influencing money and credit conditions to pursue full employment and stable prices. [34]

   The FED has done this by manipulating interest rates and the economy. And they haven't done it very well. I love the term 'free market intervention.' I believe the 'market' should be 'free' of 'intervention' by people who think they know better. We are not safer, more flexible, or more stable.

   I say we get rid of the FED and find a much better system.


- The FED manipulates interest rates

   This should be up to private banks to define their interest rates. Banks would compete for the highest saving rate and the lowest borrowing rate. Market pressures would keep these competitive.


- The FED has a monopoly on the amount of money printed

   See previous discussion above on inflation and the fix amount of currency. They have abused this before and will probably do it again (see the year 2022 for inflation).


- Audit the FED

   The FED is not accountable to anyone. It has never undergone a true comprehensive audit since it was created in 1913. [35] I think the FED should be given a forensic audit when it is 'de-funded' and 're-imagined.' The term 'Audit the FED' is sometimes a nice way of saying 'End the FED.'

## WHAT WE NEED TO COUNTER,
## TO PROTECT THE PEOPLE.

- State run Central Bank monopoly
- Fiat money
- Counterfeiting

Money isn't free, but our money must be free from the controls and manipulation by the state.

## BILL OF ADDITIONAL RIGHTS AMENDMENT

*Amendment*

*The state shall not establish or maintain a central state bank with an exclusive monopoly. The state may offer a decentralized representative currency. However, the production of the instruments of an exchange and/or legal tender shall be maintained by the state for accurate representation.*

# PLANK SIX

The Ten Planks from the Communist Manifesto 1848 by Karl Heinrich Marx & Friedrich Engels

Plank #6
Centralization of the means of communication and transportation in the hands of the state.

# WHAT IS WRONG WITH PLANK SIX?

In many countries communication and transportation are run by the state for the 'good' of the people. This has many problems. The state has no special ability to run communication or transportation operations. In many cases it's a money losing activity. Not to mention the propaganda broadcasted by the state media. The programing of the communications and destinations of the transportation are decided by a government committee and not always what the people want or need.

The first amendment was meant to cover the freedom of communications.

Amendment I

> Congress shall make no law respecting an establishment of religion, or prohibiting the free exercise thereof; or <u>abridging the freedom of speech, or of the press</u>; or the right of the people peaceably to assemble, and to petition the Government for a redress of grievances.

Even with the influence of modern technical advances, this should still cover such things as T.V., radio, internet, social media, and anything else they think up.

However, the transportation component is not covered. The horse and buggies of our past didn't lend themselves to the firm control by the state. Today we have many ways to get from here to there. Many require expensive infrastructures to support.

However, a lot of the government involvement in transportation has to do with public safety issues. I'm sure this is a good thing or at least good intentions. Which is safer: a train or a plane? How many parts in an air liner, if broke, would crash the plane? Are the quality procedures for the repair of a jet engine good enough? I do not know. At least there are government agencies who care about such things.

# WHAT ADDITIONAL CONSIDERATIONS SHOULD BE RESOLVED WITH COMMUNICATION?

- Federal Communications Commission (FCC)

  In the hay-day of radio, the FCC assigned radio frequencies to new stations. They made sure that two stations didn't overlap and had their signals fighting each other.

  Communications in the U.S. have been Regulated since the Radio Act of 1912. If you can imagine, the military, police, Fire, Ham radio and entertainment companies all wanted to be able to get their signals out over the airwaves. The Radio Act of 1912 helped to establish a commission so that the right signal got to the right audience without interference. [36]

  See below for additional comments.


- Communications Act of 1934

  The Federal Radio Commission was established in 1926 to help handle the growing radio needs of the country. Congress passed the Communications Act in 1934, to replace the Federal Radio Commission with the Federal Communications Commission (FCC). [37]

  I view the FCC as a necessary evil. If we didn't have it, chaos would ensue. With cable, internet, and satellite communications expanding everywhere somebody needs to oversee where it is all going. We don't know what the next Communications breakthroughs will be (maybe quantum entanglement) and the proper organization needs to be there to help sort it all out.

  The FCC is one of those entities that needs to be constantly monitored to insure it's not overstepping established bounds.

There is a note I need to make about 'constantly monitored' elements of the government. This is done now but only long after the fact. It's when people start finding out how the government has messed up their lives. There should be a mechanism within the government to perform this function sooner. This may be best suited for another book.

- Executive orders 11490

    This order consolidates 21 Executive orders and 2 Defense Mobilization orders. This <u>assignment of emergency preparedness functions</u> to various departments and agencies are contained and listed in Section 3015 of the order. [38]

    Sometimes drastic measures need to be taken to save lives and property in times of disasters. This is a good thing. However, if it is used to give advantage and/or money to an individual or group, then it is being abused.

- Executive orders 10999

    Executive Order 10999 -- ASSIGNING EMERGENCY PREPAREDNESS FUNCTIONS TO THE SECRETARY OF COMMERCE [39]

    This is the same but an older version of Executive orders 11490. See above.

## WHAT ADDITIONAL CONSIDERATIONS SHOULD BE RESOLVED WITH TRANSPORTATION?

- Department of Transportation (DOT)

    Anything outside of the public safety issues should be looked at carefully and removed from this department if possible. Activities like favoring and promoting one form of transportation over another is not their job. A good audit could identify these issues.

    One important activity the DOT could do is provide data and statistics on the various forms of transportation.

- Interstate Commerce Commission

    I could maybe understand this when we were a new developing country with new territories and states, but do we need it now? I think we should try to eliminate it if possible. However, I do agree that public safety issues may apply, but beyond that, I'm not sure what is necessary.

- Federal Aviation Administration

    Again, we should carefully look at and remove if possible, anything outside the scope of public safety issues.

- Federal postal monopoly

    This is not much of a monopoly with UPS and e-mail to compete with. The whole concept of a postal service is undergoing change and development.

- AMTRAK and CONRAIL and other government-owned enterprises

    The problem with Amtrak is the same as many railroads of the 20th Century. They had too much overhead costs and low revenue. Some local governments would often subsidize railroad construction to places that wouldn't pay off. Government regulation didn't help. Railroads had trouble eliminating lines where rates were often too low to be profitable. Amtrak was created to bail out the PennCentral.[40]

    Government regulations are often massive when only the safety issues are important.

    Why are we bailing out private business? Capitalism allows for business to fail, but Marxism doesn't. If it's going to fail, let it fail. We will save all that money, and someone may come along and figure out how to make it or replace it with something better. This is how we move forward and improve. If you're not allowed to fail, you are forced into stagnation.

## WHAT WE NEED TO COUNTER, TO PROTECT THE PEOPLE.

- Centralization of the means of communication
- Centralization of the means of transportation

Free speech is a good thing. Freeing the means of communication and transportation is essential.

## BILL OF ADDITIONAL RIGHTS AMENDMENT

*Amendment*

*Except in extreme national disasters or emergencies, the state shall not centralize or monopolize the means of communications and/or transportation intended for public use. The state shall not allow private elements to centralize or monopolize these means of communications and transportation. The state may operate communications and transportation for its own use or the national defense.*

# PLANK SEVEN

The Ten Planks from the Communist Manifesto 1848 by Karl Heinrich Marx & Friedrich Engels

Plank #7
Extension of factories and instruments of production owned by the state; the bringing into cultivation of waste lands, and the improvement of the soil generally in accordance with a common plan.

## WHAT IS WRONG WITH PLANK SEVEN?

I could not think of a worse situation than factories and the instruments of production run by the state. They have no skin in the game which leads to incompetent management and corruption. A company run by its owner is far more efficiently run. State run 'collective farms' have failed all over the world. They just do not work very well.

If you don't need to, why would you cultivate wasteland? Socialist must farm all the land they can because their system has seldom produced enough food to feed their populations. On the other hand, a free market can do very well.

The U.S. has one of the most efficient food production systems in the world. The total U.S. agricultural production is almost as high as China's, with a significantly smaller workforce than China. [41] The Chinese agricultural work force is almost the size of the U.S. population.

Look at this item in the plank, 'improvement of the soil generally in accordance with a <u>common plan</u>.' When I see the word 'common' in the context of Socialism, I envision a large committee sitting at a table trying to come to a consensus. That is not how you improve the soil? I may have come down a little hard on that committee because I don't trust that approach. A single farmer would seek out information from, probably more than one, wiser person. Then he would make an informed decision about <u>his</u> (skin in the game) farm.

This is one reason why a free-market system works, and a Marxist system fails.

## WHAT ADDITIONAL CONSIDERATIONS SHOULD BE RESOLVED FOR INSTRUMENTS OF PRODUCTION?

- Permits and Licenses

    Permits and licenses are prevalent throughout our government and our society. Like I said before, if these are based on safety and environmental concerns (clean air and water), I can go along with it. But it should be sensible, watched and not allowed to go too far.

- O.S.H.A. - Occupational Safety and Health Administration

  I'm all for a safe workplace. However, OSHA is a large bureaucracy and is riddled with problems.

  There are many OSHA standards that are decades old. The standards for derricks and hoists, as an example, are based on a 1943 document. What you can almost always find are situations where an employer is cited for things that are not violations. A worker named, Stefan Goulab, died from exposure to cyanide as part of a silver recovery process. It was the first time that an employer was charged with murder. However, not by OSHA, but by the District Attorney's office. [42]

  OSHA needs to be audited, streamlined, and updated to meet the true needs of industry. A simplified fact-based approach to the workplace safety is what we need in these modern times.

- Labor Boards

  An independent agency of the United States Federal Government, the National Labor Relations Board is responsible for holding the elections for many of the labor union officials and representatives. Also, the board is charged with investigating and remedying unfair labor practices. [43]

  Someone needs to be doing this to keep everybody fair. However, this is something to be closely monitored as the history of labor unions is riddled with corruption.

- Department of Commerce

  The Department of Commerce works with a variety of businesses, universities, communities, and the Nation's workers to promote job creation, economic growth, and improved standards of living. [44]

  The goals of this department sound good. However, I'm not sure how much the government should be involved. This is a very large department and should be audited often and monitored.

# WHAT ADDITIONAL CONSIDERATIONS SHOULD BE RESOLVED FOR CULTIVATION OF LAND ISSUES?

- Government involvement in agriculture, The Department of Agriculture

  This doesn't always work well. State ownership is not a successful plan.

  In Cuba the state ownership of farms has resulted in a disaster. The reason for this disaster was due to the ACP, the state-owned enterprise of CB and its monopoly over agriculture. The monopoly was established in the supply of seeds, fertilizer, and agricultural equipment. The ordinary farmer did not have the courage to enter agriculture privately. [45]

  A government intimidating farmers is not how you grow enough food to feed the people of a country. Farming needs to stay in the hands of the farmer. Perhaps the government can help in the coordination of the many elements involved in getting food to the table.

- Price support subsidies

  Governments around the world intervene in the operation of their agricultural markets. In poor third world countries, Governments routinely impose price controls to keep food prices artificially low. This will gain them favor with their more politically powerful urban residents. On the other hand, in highly developed countries the opposite occurs. Farmers use this power to seek higher prices via legislation. [46]

  This sounds like a remnant from a third world country. Whether you make the price high or low, it seems like a Marxist would love this way to control the markets. I say, "No." We should not be doing price fixing.

- Acreage allotments

  The term 'Acreage allotment' applies to a farm's acreage share, based on its previous production, and of the national acreage needed to produce sufficient supplies of a particular crop. Under the FAIR Act of 1996, the area of agriculture can be defined under provisions of this permanent commodity price support law. Acreage allotments are not applicable to crops like contract commodities, peanuts, or sugar. However, acreage allotments still apply to tobacco. [47]

What! I have no understanding as to why the government would have any authority to tell a farmer what he/she can or cannot grow. However, Marxists love this kind of control mechanism. Imagine the elites sitting around a table deciding who can grow what and how much. These people are sick.

These types of laws need to be looked at very carefully, audited, and eliminated if possible. I would think that a county or state Farmers Associations would be a better means to determine how much of what crops would be of maximum benefit for the association members. And then the farmers would have the option to follow those recommendations or not.

There is, however, one thing the government may be able to do to help the farmers. Gathering national and international statistics on crops and providing that information to the Farmers Associations so they can make better decisions.


- Land-use controls

   This is very similar to zoning laws and acreage allotments. See 'Various zoning regulations' from plank one and the previous entry for 'acreage allotments.'


- Desert Entry Act

   On March 3, 1877, the Desert Land Act was passed by the United States Congress. This encouraged and promoted the economic development of the arid and semiarid public lands in the Western states. The Act enabled individuals to apply for desert-land entry to irrigate and reclaim the land. [48]

   This could be thought of as <u>bringing into cultivation of waste lands</u>, as in the wording of the plank. The difference here is that the government is not doing the improvements. Land is being sold or provided to private citizens at a bargain for them to develop. That is the kind of thing we were doing in 1877. Do we still need to do it? I don't know and I wouldn't be opposed to it if they were still doing it.

- Environmental Protection Agency

 I believe we have a right to clean air and water. And I'm all for them doing that job. However, this is an agency that could creep into other areas. It could be possible to use this agency to condemn property or an operation for the purpose of giving an advantage to another person.

 This agency should be doing activities like monitoring toxins and pollution at all military bases here and overseas. If they need a security clearance to monitor alien poop in Area 51, then get them the clearance.

 This agency also needs to be monitored for abuse.

- Department of Interior

 In 1849, the US Department of the Interior (DOI) was established. This was to be, as one historian put it, "The Department of Everything Else." It had a wide range of duties that didn't quite fit within the purviews of the other departments. Today, the DOI manages America's lands, water, wildlife, and energy resources. [49]

 This is a very large department with a lot of different responsibilities. The DOI is not without controversy and concern.

 Following multiple reports of ethical misconduct, a House Republican is seeking an audit of the Interior Department's ethics office and senior Biden administration officials. [50]

 The DOI has a large responsibility and should be audited and monitored thoroughly and often.

- Bureau of Land Management, Bureau of Reclamation, Bureau of Mines

 What is a Bureau of government? A government bureau is an organization or office that provides services or information to the public. [51]

If this is what they are truly doing, collecting, and distributing information and providing services to the people, then it's a good thing. Problems occur when they try to change outcomes by meddling into what they are collecting data on or the services they are providing.

These Bureaus need to be watched.

- National Park Service

  We all love the National Parks and want our grand kids to grow up enjoying the beauty and history of this country. These areas need to be protected and I have no objections to this.

Looking back at these items, it may appear that I'm a little hard on some of them. Your right, I am. The people who work for these organizations work for us and for all our benefit. They are here to make everything work smoother and better. I will be the first to applaud them when that happens. However, they are not here to control, manipulate, influence, or interfere.

## WHAT WE NEED TO COUNTER, TO PROTECT THE PEOPLE.

- Instruments of production owned by the state
- Cultivation of waste lands by the state
- Improvement of the soil according to a common plan

The government doesn't know how to produce or grow anything. They need to protect those people who know how, not take it away from them.

## BILL OF ADDITIONAL RIGHTS AMENDMENT

*Amendment*

*No factories or instruments of production of products or agriculture intended for the general population shall be owned or operated by the state. The state may establish instruments or means of production or agriculture for its own use or the national defense. Also, the state may not force the cultivation of waste land or improvement of the soil.*

# PLANK EIGHT

The Ten Planks from the Communist Manifesto
1848 by Karl Heinrich Marx & Friedrich Engels

Plank #8
Equal obligation of all to work. Establishment
of Industrial armies, especially for agriculture.

# WHAT IS WRONG WITH PLANK EIGHT?

It's the word 'obligation' that bothers me. A course of action to which a person is morally or legally bound. [52] Marxists think everyone is legally bound to work. And they, the Marxist elites, will assign you a place to work and a job to do. What if that is not what you want to do? Maybe you think you can do better, or take a lesser job so you can practice your art? Well, that may be just too bad and unacceptable.

A lot of concern about this idea of 'all to work' is centered around the general concept of 'Equal Rights.' There is a difference here between the Free Society and a Marxist Society on the idea that everyone can work. In a Marxist society everyone 'shall' work. This is understandable due to their inability to provide enough for all the people. This is unlike a free society where everyone 'can' work. If you want to work, you can or you don't have too. It's up to you. If you don't want to work and be a homeless bum, you can do that. The free society seems to provide a higher standard of living then the alternatives.

# WHAT ADDITIONAL CONSIDERATIONS SHOULD BE RESOLVED?

- Social Security Administration

    The Social Security Administration (SSA) needs to be redone. A lot of new ideas have come around since the creation of the SSA. Perhaps some elements from the Singapore retirement model could help?

    The Singapore government's plan for retirees uses individual savings accounts. Both employee and employer contribute. Here the emphasis is placed on personal responsibility. Under this Singapore plan, employees contribute 20 percent of their salary to their saving account. The employers put in an additional 13 percent. The government guarantees a 2.5 percent annual return. The economics of pensions is a very subtle thing, and very, very complex. [53]

    I'm not saying this is what we should do. I would like this system to be investigated and see what in this plan is useful.

I'm sure we could come up with something similar or better that would fit our needs.

- The Department of Labor

     The Department of Labor protects the rights of workers and retirees. It also provides job training, and statistics related to working, prices, and income. [54]

     This all seems good if it is not forcing requirements that do harm. This needs to be reviewed, audited, and monitored.

- Civil Rights Act of 1964

     Under the Civil Rights Act of 1964, segregation on the grounds of race, religion or national origin was banned at all places of public accommodation. This includes courthouses, parks, restaurants, theaters, sports arenas, and hotels. This meant that no longer could minorities be denied service simply based on the color of their skin. [55]

     This law was a long time in coming. It is a shame we had to do it formally into a law. To put into law something, we should have taken for granted. The sooner we let go of all our prejudice and treat everyone by the content of their characters the better off we will all be.

- Federal Public Works Programs WPA and PWA

     WPA construction projects could cost three to four times more than the private sector. It has been labeled inefficient and a waste of taxpayers' money. Much was spent on art projects which critics deemed useless. [56]

     This sounds like the usual government waste and inefficiency. We shouldn't be doing this unless it's a 'last resort' and desperate measure.

- Affirmative Action

     Affirmative action takes positive steps in the areas of employment, education, and culture to increase the representation and involvement of both women and minorities. Historically, they have been excluded or limited in these activities. [57]

See Civil Rights Act of 1964 for my opinion.

- The Equal Rights Amendment

    I was one of the people who thought that the Equal Rights Amendment (ERA) was already law. I was wrong.

    According to the New Republic, most Americans believe the ERA already exists and that it's ancient history. [58]

    Again, see Civil Rights Act of 1964.

- Women should do all work that men do

    If the women want to! No one should be forced to do any job. Also, to deny sexual differences is not logical. See the next entry.

- Women should be eligible for the draft

    Robert A. Heinlein explained it at a basic level that goes beyond politics by saying, "Women of child-bearing age, are the ultimate treasure that we must save. Every human culture is based on 'Women and children first' - and any attempt to do it any other way leads quickly to extinction." [59]

    In my opinion we should not draft women. This doesn't mean that women can't volunteer for non-combative rolls in the military. They have distinguished themselves well in a long history of service to this country.

    At this time, I will not entertain any fantasy WOK ideas.

## WHAT WE NEED TO COUNTER, TO PROTECT THE PEOPLE.

- Obligation of all to work
- Establishment of Industrial armies
- Forced labor
- Woman eligible for the draft

This is simple. We are not here to work for the government, the government is here to work for us.

## BILL OF ADDITIONAL RIGHTS AMENDMENT

*Amendment*

*Section 1.*

*All people have the right to pursue whatever legal occupation they choose. Unless a person has been convicted of a crime or incarcerated, no one shall be forced to labor by any Federal, State, or local governments.*

*Section 2.*

*Women shall not be forced into the draft to serve in the military but can volunteer for military service.*

# PLANK NINE

The Ten Planks from the Communist Manifesto
1848 by Karl Heinrich Marx & Friedrich Engels

Plank #9
Combination of agriculture with manufacturing
industries; gradual abolition of the distinction
between town and country by a more equable
distribution of the population over the country.

# WHAT IS WRONG WITH PLANK NINE?

Why would anyone force agriculture and manufacturing industries together? Marx might have thought it would be efficient to do so. But it is not up to the government. If a company evaluates their operation and finds a benefit to combine agriculture and manufacturing, then they could do that, or not. That company would know better than anyone if they should do it.

Guess what? If that company makes a mistake and it doesn't work, only they will fail. In a Fascist or Communist system everyone would suffer because the combining would be adopted system wide. A mistake like that, and countries could starve.

Because of an increasingly productive farming sector, the U.S. is one of the most efficient food producers. Many American companies dominate the food export markets. [60]

A free and privately owned agricultural system is always the best approach.

What is wrong with town and country? Some people like the small towns and others like big cities and still others like the quiet countryside. With some exception like, 'We tested atom bombs here and it's still hot,' or 'This is private property, and you can't live here,' it is not up to anyone to tell us where we can or cannot live. We have the freedom to choose and not be assigned where to live.

What is even more shocking to me, is the Marxism view that someone could tell us what we will be eating.

If you don't want to starve, you'll eat weeds and bugs and drink toilet water, own nothing and you'll like it. They believe that through media manipulation, you and I can be conditioned to eat and drink things that are now considered nauseating. [61]

What! No more Saturday Bar-B-Q? I love the way they think we can be brainwashed to go along with all of this. Is this the Marxist future you are looking forward to?

# WHAT ADDITIONAL CONSIDERATIONS SHOULD BE RESOLVED?

- Planning Reorganization Act of 1949

   Congress can temporarily extend to the President of the United States the Presidential reorganization authority. This major statutory power permits the president to divide, consolidate, abolish, or create agencies of the U.S. federal government by presidential directive. These are subject to limited legislative oversight. [62]

   This may be fine if limited to government agencies only. This power should not be applied to private holdings or business.


- Zoning (Title 17 1910-1990)

   As I have said before, zoning laws are usually intended to organize a developing city. Can it be used to obtain property? I'm sure it has and that would be unacceptable and should be considered illegal.


- Public 'law' 89-136

   This law was to provide grants for public works and development of facilities, other financial assistance. It was also to provide coordination needed to alleviate conditions of substantial and persistent unemployment and underemployment in economically distressed areas. [63]

   This all sounds good. However, if people are forced to work or move where they don't want to, it is wrong.

   Unemployment and underemployment are a problem that is often caused by the government, and this is their feeble attempt to correct the mistake. Addressing the root cause by finding out the reason why this is happening and correcting the problem is always the best approach.

- Super Corporate Farms

Corporate farming is the practice of large-scale agriculture on farms owned or influenced by large companies. Nine US states have enacted laws that prohibit or restrict corporate farming. These laws can target a corporation's use of the land. In some cases, a company can own but not farm the land. They may outright prohibit corporations from buying or owning farmland. [64]

To say that a person or company can or cannot own a piece of land seems wrong to me. However, this may best be decided by the individual states who have a better understanding of their land and are stake holders in its future.

## WHAT WE NEED TO COUNTER, TO PROTECT THE PEOPLE.

- Combination of agriculture with manufacturing industries
- Forced equable distribution of the population
- Assigning people to live in a particular place or region

The government should be defending our rights to do what we want, not telling us where and how to live.

## BILL OF ADDITIONAL RIGHTS AMENDMENT

*Amendment*

*Federal, State, or local governments shall not force the combining of industrial production and agriculture.*

*Federal, State, or local governments shall not force a person to live in a designated place unless a person has been convicted of a crime and is confined to a detention location.*

# PLANK TEN

The Ten Planks from the Communist Manifesto
1848 by Karl Heinrich Marx & Friedrich Engels

Plank #10
Free education for all children in government
schools. Abolition of children's factory labor
in its present form. Combination of education
with industrial production, etc. etc.

# WHAT IS WRONG WITH PLANK TEN?

This plank is a tough one for me. I believe in education and the idea that it improves the community and the country. I was raised in the public education system, and it seemed to work well when I was there. So, what is wrong with public schools?

In late 2021 there was a widespread but peaceful revolt against government schools. The disagreement was over who has the right to determine what is taught and whom the Board of Education is responsible to. The Marxist leaning public officials said that they had those rights; yet the mothers and fathers thought they had the rights.

What difference does it make who decides? The simple reason is that the parents did not want their children brainwashed and turned into good little Marxist children. A government should not have access to the spongy minds of our children.

In the mid-2022, during the writing of this book, many programs were in place in many cities to teach sexual education to grade school children. Is this what you want for your school age child to be taught at school? I think the parent, should have the choice to decide.

If the parents don't have the right to make these choices, then no one does. 'My child, my responsibility.' It doesn't belong to the state. Private, church, and home schools are benefitting in a big way from this disagreement over education.

What about Charter Schools? Charter Schools are not held to some of the same laws, regulations, and guidelines as regular public schools. Although they are not allowed to charge tuition, they often have <u>controlled enrollments and waiting lists</u> for students wanting to attend. [65]

Charter Schools do not seem to be the answer for everyone. Currently there is talk of 'the money following the child.' [66] Another term is, 'School vouchers.' The idea is that taxpayers' money assigned to education was divided up between the children. Each child is given a voucher for his or her money. The amount of money would depend on such things as location and age of the child. The voucher is then given to the school they have chosen to attend, and it pays for their education. This should even apply to home schooling.

This would unleash the competitive edge of the business of education in a free market economy. Schools would strive to do better to attract more customers . . . I mean, students.

Nobel Prize-winning economist Milton Friedman, PhD, a champion of the free market, argued for school vouchers back in 1955. He said that vouchers would result in a 'great widening in the educational opportunities open to our children.' [67]

The idea of combining of education with industrial production is as repulsive as it sounds, considering the Marxist intent to have children in industry. The child would learn a skill, on the job that the child would have for the rest of its life. We have child labor laws, to prevent abusive treatment of children in these conditions. Remember, this plank is meant for industrial production, not making smart kids. To a Marxist, production is more important than people. This would not apply to things like a shop class at school or an internship or that summer job to earn extra money. The 'summer job' can be an education onto itself.

## WHAT ADDITIONAL CONSIDERATIONS SHOULD BE RESOLVED?

- The Department of Education

  The federal governments' Department of Education could be re-imagined as a kind of feedback to the states, school districts and individual schools. Which school is doing the best in a district or the best school in a state? Schools could improve their performance and quality of education by following what worked well in other schools. The Department of Education could be a great unbiased source of information and statistics on the emerging private schools.

- The National Education Association

  How would this change? I'm not sure how this would change, but there would still be work for it to do.

- Teachers Unions

    Teachers would continue to have the right to unionize.

- Private and church schools must have permits, licenses, and approved curriculum

    Who regulates that now, and who determines the private school's curriculum? The states regulate the private schools. I would like to see all private schools have a system whereby parents could formally monitor and input their ideas for changes to the requirements and curriculum. This could go a long way to an improvement in education along with the information and statistics from the new Department of Education.

- Is a voucher system constitutional?

    In 2002, the US Supreme Court upheld the constitutionality of Ohio's Cleveland Scholarship Program. In this case Zelman v. Simmons-Harris, the ruling held that the voucher program did not violate the Establishment Clause of the First Amendment or the use of vouchers for religious schools. [68]

    So, we already know that a voucher system is compatible with the Constitution.

- Child Labor Laws

    We already have child labor laws preventing children from working in industry at too young an age.

## WHAT WE NEED TO COUNTER, TO PROTECT THE PEOPLE.

- Government owned and operated schools

The government has no expertise in teaching, so leave it up to professionals.

# BILL OF ADDITIONAL RIGHTS AMENDMENT

*Amendment*

*Federal, State, or local governments shall not establish or maintain schools for public education. The state may, however, provide funds to the students for their education through a voucher system.*

# COMBINING PLANKS
# FOR AMENDMENTS

Some of these planks are very similar. I think the finished amendments should combine those similar planks, where it makes sense.

At the time of this writing there are twenty-seven amendments to the Constitution. I'm labeling the proposed amendments as X+1 through X+5. The "X," of course, is twenty-seven, or the number of the last amendment to the Constitution.

# COMBINE ELEMENTS TO PROTECT THE PEOPLE
## PLANKS 1 AND 4

From Plank 1

- 'Eminent domain'
- 'Forfeiture' provisions
- Abolishment of private property

From Plank 4

- Confiscation of the property from emigrants
- Confiscation of the property from rebels

# ADDITIONAL RIGHTS AMENDMENT
## TO REPLACE ONE AND FOUR

*The right to own property.*

*Amendment X+1*

*Section 1.*

*Federal, State, and local governments or their agencies shall not interfere with the right to keep and own properties, or abolish, confiscate, or under 'forfeiture' provisions obtain private property of citizens or immigrants or criminals without due process and only if the property has been proven to be involved in an illegal act.*

*Section 2.*

*Federal, State, and local governments or their agencies shall not use 'eminent domain' to obtain property for private use. It must be for government use only, and paid for at fair market prices. If the property is not used for the original declared government purpose within four years, the property is returned to the previous owner without charge.*

## COMBINE ELEMENTS TO PROTECT THE PEOPLE PLANKS 2 AND 3

From Plank 2

- Progressive income tax
- Graduated income tax

From Plank 3

- Taxation of inheritance
- Abolition of inheritance
- Abolition to give an inheritance
- Abolition to get an inheritance
- Lack of legal Obligations of inheritance

## ADDITIONAL RIGHTS AMENDMENT TO REPLACE TWO AND THREE

*The right to far taxation.*

*Amendment X+2*

*Section 1.*

*No Federal, State, or local governments shall establish a progressive or graduated tax.*

*Section 2.*

*No seizure or taxation or abolition of the rights to give or receive inheritance shall be made without due process and only if it is involved in an illegal act.*

# COMBINE ELEMENTS TO PROTECT THE PEOPLE PLANKS 5, 6 AND 10

From Plank 5

- State run Central Bank monopoly
- Fiat money
- Counterfeiting

From Plank 6

- Centralization of the means of communication
- Centralization of the means of transportation

From Plank 10

- Government own and operated schools

# ADDITIONAL RIGHTS AMENDMENT TO REPLACE FIVE, SIX AND TEN

*The right to be free from government monopoly.*

*Amendment X+3*

*Section 1.*

*Except in extreme national disasters or emergencies, the state shall not centralize or monopolize a state bank, means of communications, means of transportation and/or establish and maintain schools intended for public use.*

*Section 2.*

*The state may offer a decentralized representative currency. The production of the instruments of an exchange and/or legal tender shall be maintained by the state for accurate representation.*

*Section 3.*

*The state shall not allow private elements to centralize or monopolize the means of communications and transportation. The state may operate communications and transportation for its own use or the national defense.*

*Section 4.*

*The state may provide funds to students for their education through a voucher system.*

## COMBINE ELEMENTS TO PROTECT THE PEOPLE
## PLANKS 7 AND 9

From Plank 7

- Instruments of production owned by the state
- Cultivation of waste lands by the state
- Improvement of the soil according to a common plan

From Plank 9

- Combination of agriculture with manufacturing industries
- Forced equable distribution of the population
- Assigning people to live in a particular place or region

## ADDITIONAL RIGHTS AMENDMENT TO REPLACE
## SEVEN AND NINE

*The freedom to live and work.*

*Amendment X+4*

*Section 1.*

*No factories or instruments of production of products or agriculture intended for the general population shall be owned or operated by the state. Federal, State, and local governments shall not force the combining of industrial production and agriculture. The state may establish instruments or means of production or agriculture for its own use or the national defense. Also, the state may not force the cultivation of waste land or improvement of the soil.*

*Section 2.*

*Federal, State, or local governments cannot force a person to live in a designated place unless a person has been convicted of a crime and is confined to a detention location.*

# ELEMENTS TO PROTECT THE PEOPLE PLANK 8

From Plank 8

- Obligation of all to work
- Establishment of Industrial armies
- Forced labor
- Women eligible for the draft

Except for the number assigned to this Amendment, the Plank 8 Amendment has not changed. This one will not be combined with any other.

*The freedom not to work.*

*Amendment X+5*

*Section 1.*

*All people have the right to pursue whatever legal occupation they choose. Unless a person has been convicted of a crime or incarcerated, no one shall be forced to labor by any Federal, State, or local governments.*

*Section 2.*

*Women shall not be forced into the draft to serve in the military but can volunteer for military service.*

## BILL OF ADDITIONAL RIGHTS

So here they are, five amendments to add to the Constitution. There is, of course, no guarantee that they alone will keep the Socialist wolf at bay. It will always take freedom-loving people and judges to keep America on the right course. The point is that when the Bill of Rights was created two hundred years ago there was no 'Socialism.' And two hundred years from now there may be something new just as bad, if not worse. Hopefully, someone in that future will go through this again. Thank our Founding Fathers for amendments.

# IS THIS THE END?

That was the easy part but not the end. The hard part would be to try to hammer out the exact wording. You know, something we could all agree on. Sometimes it's hard to get two people to agree on anything, like what to eat for dinner. And then the next-to-impossible task would be of implementing five amendments to the constitution at the same time. It seems like to do just one would be a herculean task.

Personally, I would be happy if any one of them would be adopted. I have my favorites; do you have one or more that you would like to see adopted to the Constitution?

I could make the argument that if we don't do this, there would not be a free USA in the future. But I would be cheating. The fact is I don't know the future. No one does.

This is what I do know. The Marxist and Fascist want this control. You remember, the plank's one through ten. I don't want the Marxist and Fascist anywhere near our freedoms and liberty. If they say they want it, I say don't let them have it. We can flourish with these five Amendments and the Marxist and Fascist can't. They don't know how.

You can appose or argue the merits of these ideas all you want. Good or bad, I feel strongly about them. It's not so much this-ism or that-ism which has me concerned. It's the sheer body count that haunts me and makes me angry and afraid. And that is my real concern about this country. You can't ignore the hundred million deaths because of Socialism in the last century. To do so would be like ignoring on-coming traffic.

I didn't say much about the Marxist themselves, the people that do these terrible things. I'm talking about the masses, the common folk or the 'useful idiots,' as the elites (or bandits) call them. I will be kind and consider them ignorant and not stupid. Although, I'm sure that Carlo Cipolla[69] would consider them stupid because they (the useful idiots) would be just as hurt (and dead) as everyone else.

This is where preventing and reversing Plank 10, government schools, from happening becomes so important. Not teaching our children what is important is just as bad as teaching them the wrong things. If the 'useful idiots' were taught well when they were children, maybe they would be useful to themselves and others, and not idiots.

I just heard that Florida has a 'Victims of Communism Memorial Day' in their schools every November 7th. A great first step in teaching our children well.

I would also like to leave you with one last quote from my good friend. I think he sums it all up well. He captures what I've been trying to say.

"Socialism is and works kind of like a social disease."

Melvin Entwhistle

This may not be exactly what I meant, but I think you get the idea.

Will all this cure Marxism? Some would say that we could just pass a law, leave it up to the states. We just don't need an amendment. It wouldn't be the same. These five amendments may not stop the Mass Formation psychosis that would lead us to totalitarianism. But it could help America to remain free for many years. After all, this is only the beginning.

How many million American deaths could you tolerate before you think Marxism might be a bad idea? Five million, ten million, maybe twenty million would get your attention? We know that freedom and liberty work. We must maximize the freedom that works, as much as we can stand, and flee as far away as possible from the Marxism that kills people. If you think that is too extreme, history is not on your side. Remember the 100 million dead?

These Amendments would weave this determination against this evil into the fabric of the constitution and would couple it to our very being as a nation. That is what the Bill of Rights has become. No matter how they try to pass bills and tweak laws, the Bill of Rights is still the conscience and soul of the American people in written form. And in my opinion, the Bill of Additional Rights should also be part of that fabric and soul.

## THE END

# NOTES


1. "Socialism", Merriam-Webster, © 2022 Merriam-Webster, Incorporated https://www.merriam-webster.com/dictionary/socialism

2. "Socialism is the philosophy of failure, the creed of ignorance, and the gospel of envy." —Perth, Scotland, 28 May 1948, in Churchill, Europe Unite: Speeches 1947 & 1948 (London: Cassell, 1950), 347. https://winstonchurchill.hillsdale.edu/socialism-is-the-philosophy-of-failure-winston-churchill/

3. "WHY MARXISM FAILED, FAILS, AND WILL ALWAYS FAIL", EL RINCÓN DEL PARQUET, Leer más:2015, Todos los derechos reservados. https://www.elrincondelparquet.com/news/why-marxism-failed-fails-and-will-always-fail/Leer más:

4. Why The World Should Not Forget About Pol Pot, The Brutal Cambodian Dictator, By Richard Stockton, Checked By John Kuroski, Published December 29, 2021, Updated January 11, 2022 https://allthatsinteresting.com/pol-pot

5. "The Basic Laws of Human Stupidity" - URV, Carlo M. Cipolla, Whole Earth Review. Spring 1987 p 2 - 7) gandalf.fee.urv.cat/professors/AntonioQuesada/Curs1920/Cipolla_laws.pdf

6. WHAT IS A USEFUL IDIOT?, TOUCH STONE CONNECT, March 25, 2022, by pensiamentopeligroso https://touchstoneconnect.com/2022/03/25/what-is-a-useful-idiot/

7. "Norman Thomas Quotes and Sayings", Norman Thomas 1944, Copyright © 2022 Inspiring Quotes, American socialist https://www.inspiringquotes.us/author/1660-norman-thomas

8. "The Ten Planks of the Communist Manifesto", BY TS on AUGUST 5, 2016, Laissez-Faire Republic http://www.laissez-fairerepublic.com/TenPlanks.html

9. "Eminent Domain", Investopedia, By WILL KENTON, Updated August 24, 2021, Reviewed by MICHAEL J BOYLE, Fact checked by KATRINA MUNICHIELLO
https://www.investopedia.com/terms/e/eminent-domain.asp

10. "Eminent Domain", KENTON, Updated August 24, 2021,
https://www.investopedia.com/terms/e/eminent-domain.asp

11. The Holy Bible, New International Version, Copyright 1978 by New York International Bible Society

12. "PRIVATE PROPERTY RIGHTS DEFINED", TOM DEWEESE, 11/7/2012
https://americanpolicy.org/2012/11/07/private-property-rights-defined/

13. "Eminent Domain", KENTON, Updated August 24, 2021,
https://www.investopedia.com/terms/e/eminent-domain.asp

14. "Usurp", WordPerfect 2021, Dictionary "Oxford University Press"

15. "Racketeer Influenced and Corrupt Organizations Act (RICO)", Legal Information from Nolo, 2022
https://www.nolo.com/legal-encyclopedia/content/rico-act.html

16. "National Environmental Policy Act", NEPA.GOV, NEPAnet web site.
https://ceq.doe.gov/index.html

17. "Tariff in United States history", From Wikipedia, 2020
https://en.wikipedia.org/wiki/Tariff_in_United_States_history

18. "Flat Tax", Article by Wallstreetmojo Editorial Team, Reviewed by Dheeraj Vaidya, CFA, FRM
https://www.wallstreetmojo.com/flat-tax/

19. What Are Inheritance Taxes?, Turbo Tax, Written by a TurboTax Expert, Reviewed by a TurboTax CPA, Updated for Tax Year 2021 / October 16, 2021 07:25 AM
https://turbotax.intuit.com/tax-tips/estates/what-are-inheritance-taxes/L93IUc3sC

20. What Are Inheritance Taxes?, Written by TurboTax, https://turbotax.intuit.com/tax-tips/estates/what-are-inheritance-taxes/L93IUc3sC

21. "Congress Should Protect Americans from Unjust Property Seizure", COMMENTARY Economic And Property Rights - The Heritage Foundation, Nov 29th, 2017, originally appeared in The Daily Signal, By Jason Snead, Krista Chavez
https://www.heritage.org/economic-and-property-rights/commentary/congress-should-protect-americans-unjust-property-seizure

22. Money Laundering Control Act, From Wikipedia, last edited on 2 December 2021, at 07:16 (UTC)
https://en.wikipedia.org/wiki/Money_Laundering_Control_Act

23. "Understanding a Federal Tax Lien", IRS, Page Last Reviewed or Updated: 02-Jun-2021
https://www.irs.gov/businesses/small-businesses-self-employed/understanding-a-federal-tax-lien

24. "Understanding a Federal Tax Lien", IRS
https://www.irs.gov/businesses/small-businesses-self-employed/understanding-a-federal-tax-lien

25. "What do I need to place a lien against someones property?", RealEstateLawyers, Nolo, 2022
https://www.realestatelawyers.com/legal-advice/real-estate/property-liens/what-i-need-place-lien-against-someones-property

26. Is The Fed Unconstitutional?, Valentin Schmid, Edwin Vieira Jr., June 28, 2014 Updated: January 19, 2016
https://www.theepochtimes.com/is-the-fed-unconstitutional_763988.html?welcomeuser=1

27. "11 reasons why the Federal Reserve is bad", Reprinted with permission, http://theeconomiccollapseblog.com, 01 March 2011
https://www.michaeljournal.org/articles/banks/item/11-reasons-why-the-federal-reserve-is-bad

28. MONETARY POLICY FEDERAL RESERVE, Federal Reserve Note, By LAURA GREEN, Updated June 14, 2021

29. "Fiat vs. Representative Money: What's the Difference?", By THE INVESTOPEDIA TEAM, Fact checked by SUZANNE KVILHAUG, Reviewed by SOMER ANDERSON on September 14, 2021
https://www.investopedia.com/ask/answers/041615/what-difference-between-fiat-money-and-representative-money.asp#:~:text=Fiat%20money%20is%20physical%20money%E2%80%94both%20paper%20money%20and,fiat%20and%20representative%20money%20are%20backed%20by%20something.

30. "Invisible Hand", By CHRISTINA MAJASKI, Reviewed by MICHAEL SONNENSHEIN, Fact checked by ARIEL COURAGE, Updated September 28, 2020
https://www.investopedia.com/terms/i/invisiblehand.asp

31. "COUNTERFEITING IN THE OLD WEST", By Vicki Hunt Budge, Posted by Caroline Clemmons, Sweethearts of the West, 2/02/2020,

https://sweetheartsofthewest.blogspot.com/2020/02/counterfeiting-in-old-west.html

32. "Fiat vs. Representative Money: What's the Difference?" INVESTOPEDIA TEAM

https://www.investopedia.com/ask/answers/041615/what-difference-between-fiat-money-and-representative-money.asp#:~:text=Fiat%20money%20is%20physical%20money%E2%80%94both%20paper%20money%20and,fiat%20and%20representative%20money%20are%20backed%20by%20something.

33. US Debt Clock.org, March 23, 2022
https://usdebtclock.org/#

34. "What is and the purpose of the Federal Reserve Act?", Microsoft BING, www.federalreserve.gov/faqs/about_12594.htm
https://www.bing.com/search?q=The+Federal+Reserve+Act&cvid=702066c740004911bae4624aa6435796&aqs=edge..69i57.8036j0j1&FORM=ANNTA1&PC=DCTS

35. "11 reasons why the Federal Reserve is bad", Reprinted with permission, http://theeconomiccollapseblog.com, 01 March 2011
https://www.michaeljournal.org/articles/banks/item/11-reasons-why-the-federal-reserve-is-bad

36. "The History of the Federal Communications Commission", Mitel Networks Corp, 2021
https://www.mitel.com/articles/history-federal-communications-commission-fcc

37. "The History of the Federal Communications Commission", Mitel
https://www.mitel.com/articles/history-federal-communications-commission-fcc

38. "Executive Order 11490 -- Assigning emergency preparedness functions to Federal departments and agencies", Richard Nixon, October 28, 1969.
https://www.disastercenter.com/laworder/11490.htm

39. "Executive Order 10999 -- ASSIGNING EMERGENCY PREPAREDNESS FUNCTIONS TO THE SECRETARY OF COMMERCE", JOHN F. KENNEDY, February 16, 1962.
https://www.disastercenter.com/laworder/10999.htm

40. "WHAT IS AMTRAK'S PROBLEM?", Noel T. Braymer, July 15, 2012, The Rail Passenger Association of California, aka RailPAC, is a division of non-profit Citizens For Rail California, Inc. (CRC), dba Rail Passenger Association of California.

https://railpac.org/2012/07/15/what-is-amtraks-problem/

41. "4 Countries That Produce the Most Food", Investopedia, By SEAN ROSS Updated April 29, 2021, Reviewed by MICHAEL J BOYLE https://www.investopedia.com/articles/investing/100615/4-countries-produce-most-food.asp

42. "OSHA: The Good, the Bad and the Ugly", EHS Today, Contributing Editor John F. Rekus, PE, MS, CIH, CSP, Sept. 30, 2001 https://www.ehstoday.com/archive/article/21914339/osha-the-good-the-bad-and-the-ugly

43. "What you should know about the Labor Board", LAWS, Modified date: December 22, 2019 https://employment.laws.com/what-you-should-know-about-the-labor-board#:~:text=Labor%20Board%20Quick%20Facts%3A%201%20The%20national%20labor,Liebman%3B%20the%20agency%20operates%20with%20nearly%201%2C650%20employees

44. U.S. Department of Commerce, USA.gov, https://www.usa.gov/federal-agencies/u-s-department-of-commerce

45. "Why did the peasants resist the collective farms?", Alex Dopico, 07/13/2020, https://janetpanic.com/why-did-the-peasants-resist-the-collective-farms/#Why_did_the_peasants_resist_the_collective_farms

46. "The Concise Encyclopedia of Economics", Agricultural Price Supports, by Robert L. Thompson https://www.econlib.org/library/Enc1/AgriculturalPriceSupports.html

47. "Acreage allotment", Author: Mark McCracken, TeachMeFinance.com http://www.teachmefinance.com/Scientific_Terms/Acreage%20allotment%20.html

48. "Desert Land Act Facts", KidsKonnect, April 29, 2019, https://kidskonnect.com/history/desert-land-act/

49. "US Department of the Interior Overview",   Glassdoor, https://www.glassdoor.com/Overview/Working-at-US-Department-of-the-Interior-EI_IE33310.11,40.htm

50. "Top Republican demands audit of Interior Department ethics office", Washington Examiner, by Andrew Kerr, Investigative Reporter, January 24, 2022 03:54 PM https://www.washingtonexaminer.com/news/top-republican-demands-audit-of-interior-department-ethics-office

51. "what does a us bureau do", Microsoft BING

https://www.bing.com/search?q=Bureau+of&cvid=831a055a884c410e8
3c9cf2fc909b67e&aqs=edge..69i57.2101j0j1&FORM=ANNTA1&PC
=DCTS

52. WordPerfect 2021, Dictionary, Oxford University Press

53. "Singapore's retirement system worth studying", By Michael A. Lev, The
Seattle Times, Copyright © 2021, Originally published March 20, 2005
at 12:00 am,
https://www.seattletimes.com/business/singapores-retirement-
system-worth-studying/#:~:text=The%20Singapore%20
government%E2%80%99s%20plan%20for%20retirees%20uses%20
individual,which%20most%20do%2C%20or%20to%20pay%20
for%20education.

54. "US Department of Labor, What the DOL Does for You", KIMBERLY
AMADEO, Updated February 26, 2022, REVIEWED BY ERIC
ESTEVEZ
FACT CHECKED BY HANS JASPERSON
https://www.thebalance.com/u-s-department-of-labor-
3305991#:~:text=The%20U.S.%20Department%20of%20Labor%20
%28DOL%29%20is%20a,provides%20statistics%20related%20
to%20working%2C%20prices%2C%20and%20income.

55. "Civil Rights Act of 1964", Author History.com Editors, HISTORY,
A&E Television Networks, JAN 4, 2010
https://www.history.com/topics/black-history/civil-rights-act

56. "Works Progress Administration (WPA)", By DANIEL LIBERTO,
Published October 13, 2021
https://www.investopedia.com/works-progress-administration-wpa-
definition-5204419

57. "Affirmative Action", Stanford Encyclopedia of Philosophy, Robert
Fullinwider, revision Mon Apr 9, 2018
https://plato.stanford.edu/entries/affirmative-action/

58. "16 Facts and Figures About the Equal Rights Amendment", Jeff Bogle,
Readers Digest, Updated: Jul. 14, 2021,
https://www.rd.com/article/equal-rights-amendment/

59. "Speech at the Naval Academy on patriotism, 1973", Robert A Heinlein,
My Daily Kona, TUESDAY, OCTOBER 20, 2015, Posted by Mr.
Garabaldi,
https://mydailykona.blogspot.com/2015/10/robert-heinlein-speech-to-
usna-1973.html

60. "4 Countries That Produce the Most Food", Investopedia, By SEAN ROSS Updated April 29, 2021, Reviewed by MICHAEL J BOYLE https://www.investopedia.com/articles/investing/100615/4-countries-produce-most-food.asp

61. "World Economic Forum: We Can be "Conditioned" to Eat Weeds and Bugs to Save Us From Climate Change.", by James Murphy, The New American, December 3, 2020
https://thenewamerican.com/world-economic-forum-we-can-be-conditioned-to-eat-weeds-and-bugs-to-save-us-from-climate-change/

62. "Presidential reorganization authority", Wikipedia,
https://en.wikipedia.org/wiki/Presidential_reorganization_authority#:~:text=The%20Reorganization%20Act%20of%201949%20was%20the%20last,plan%20as%20its%20own%20kind%20of%20presidential%20directive.

63. "PUBLIC LAW 89-136", "Public Works and Economic Development Act of 1965", AUG. 26 1965
https://uscode.house.gov/statutes/pl/89/136.pdf

64. "Corporate farming", From Wikipedia,
https://en.wikipedia.org/wiki/Corporate_farming

65. "What are the Pros and Cons of Charter Schools?", ThoughtCo, By Derrick Meador, Updated on April 15, 2018
https://www.thoughtco.com/what-are-the-pros-and-cons-of-a-charter-school-3194629

66. "SCHOOL Act Would Assure Education Money 'Follows the Child, Not the System'", DR. SUSAN BERRY21, Aug 2020, Breitbart News Network,
https://www.breitbart.com/politics/2020/08/21/school-act-would-assure-education-money-follows-the-child-not-the-system/

67. "School Vouchers – Top 4 Pros and Cons", Author: ProCon.org, 11/19/2020
https://www.procon.org/headlines/school-vouchers-top-4-pros-and-cons/

68. "School Vouchers – Top 4 Pros and Cons", ProCon.org, 11/19/2020
https://www.procon.org/headlines/school-vouchers-top-4-pros-and-cons/

69. "The Basic Laws of Human Stupidity" - URV, Carlo M. Cipolla, Whole Earth Review. Spring 1987 p 2 - 7)
gandalf.fee.urv.cat/professors/AntonioQuesada/Curs1920/Cipolla_laws.pdf